Please return/renew this item by the last date shown.
Library items may also be renewed by phone on
030 33 33 1234 (24hours) or via our website

www.cumbria.gov.uk/libraries

Cumbria Libraries

CLIC
Interactive Catalogue

Ask for a CLIC password

Also out:

Spangles McNasty and the Fish of Gold

Spangles McNasty and the Tunnel of Doom

Spangles McNasty and the Diamond Skull

Steve Webb

Illustrated by

Chris Mould

ANDERSEN PRESS • LONDON

First published in Great Britain in 2018 by
Andersen Press Limited
20 Vauxhall Bridge Road
London SW1V 2SA
www.andersenpress.co.uk

2 4 6 8 10 9 7 5 3 1

British Library Cataloguing in Publication Data available.

ISBN 978 1 78344 638 4

Printed and bound in Great Britain by
Clays Limited, Bungay, Suffolk, NR35 1ED

For Scary Mary

SW

For Spangles fans everywhere

CM

The List

Spangles McNasty was as grumpy as a walnut with a face to match. 'Who likes **walnuts** anyway?' he moaned, lost in thought. 'No one, that's who, not even walnut trees.'

He was rarely found in a good mood, in fact he was more likely to be found farting in the library.

'There's nothin' like a **good trump** down

the **science-fiction end**,' he said as he sulked along Bitterly High Street with his best friend and **collecting** accomplice, Sausage-face Pete.

But even the mention of one of his favourite hobbies didn't raise his spirits. Spangles had the shopping glooms, big time.

Sausage-face Pete sang awfully, in an attempt to cheer him up.

'The sun has got his hat on, hip hip hip hooray!'

The sun shone down on Spangles and Sausage-face Pete, and wondered what they were up to and also what sort of hat it would like if it could have a hat, which it couldn't. It decided a fireproof one would be best and even more quickly concluded it was unlikely it would ever have a cold head.

'You **sure** you couldn't have just done the shoppin' bit **without** me, Sausage?' Spangles grumbled, although in reality he knew Sausage-face Pete couldn't be trusted with anything more complicated than 'Which welly goes where?' He even got *that* wrong half the time and put his bright yellow wellies on the wrong feet. Sometimes not even his own.

'Oh flip to the flops,' Spangles sighed, remembering how important the **MARBLES** bit of the shopping business was. 'They do 'ave to be just right I suppose,' he admitted. Then he spotted an interesting distraction approaching.

'WHO'S A TINY BABY THEN?!'

he suddenly yelled at a baby in a pushchair.

The baby **giggled** in response, but the old lady pushing the pushchair **tutted** dismissively at Spangles, who replied by pulling the silliest face he could right back at her.

'Ahh, **that's better**, Sausage. Flippin' shoppin' list's got me **right stressed**,' Spangles said, screwing up the tiny list of only two items:

shopping list

1. Marbles
2. Parrot

Spangles relaxed a little. He poked the screwed-up list into a passing ice cream while its licker wasn't looking.

Seeing Bitterly Library ahead, he suddenly ran off, his long pin-stripe-suited legs gangling him up the library steps like a baldy pelican. 'Just time for a quickie!' he yelled back as he disappeared through the revolving doors only to reappear almost instantly, laughing like a hyena in a tickling contest.

'Better?' Sausage asked.

'Fart-tastic, Sausage!'

Spangles beamed.

'Fart-tastic.'

PaaarP!

Spangles had another list, which had nothing to do with shopping and everything to do with being nasty. It was a list of his top five favourite nasties, all of which he tried to do every day.

'That's the **shoutin' at babies, pullin' faces at old ladies** and **farting in the library** ticked off my nasty list!' He grinned happily as he scooped up a handful of cold greasy chips from a bin and stuffed them into his mouth. **'An'** nom-nom-nom – **the** – mmm – **eatin'** – nom-nom – **cold chips from bins**,' he added, and burped noisily at another passing baby.

Sausage stopped in front of a large shop window. *Bert's Bits – for all your bits*, a sign boasted above the door. 'That just leaves the collectin' other people's spangly things, then, me old happy jack,' Sausage said.

'Ahh yes, me topper-most fave nasty of all,' Spangles replied dreamily, as he joined Sausage at the window. His greedy eyes quickly found several large jars of **MARBLES**. He grinned madly at the cheap glass balls and thought of the enormous riches he was convinced he would soon be 'collecting', or 'stealing' as dictionaries always spell it.

'Righty-ho, Sausage, I'll get them beauties, you get the parrot and the you-know-what, and I'll meet you back at your boat. And don't forget your disguise!' Spangles waited nervously, knowing it would be a small miracle if Sausage remembered the plan, the whole plan and nothing but the plan – or in fact, any of it.

Sausage heaved a heavy tin of black paint from the left pocket of his bright yellow fisherman's mac and a large brush from the right. 'I got it covered, me old slapdash,' he replied with a wink.

Spangles was still worried. 'And the beard?' he asked, tugging Sausage's fish-stinky fake beard by the elastic that attached it to his oversized bright yellow fisherman's hat.

Sausage-face Pete slipped his brush-holding hand back into his right pocket, and fished out a bushy blue beard. 'A sailor is always prepared,' he said, and walked away towards the promenade.

Spangles stepped into Bert's Bits. It was almost empty and almost closing time. **'Hello, Bert,'** he said as politely as he knew how to the young lady behind the counter. She merely stared back at him, chewing gum loudly.

'I've come for **some bits**,' Spangles added, struggling with the politeness business already and resisting the urge to shout, **'Bert, you look like a girl!'**

Spotting some jars of jam at the distant back of the shop, he added, **'Bits of jam.'**

The girl, whose name was not even nearly Bert but actually Frankie, flicked her eyes briefly to the jam and back, and blew a bubble slowly until it popped.

'Would you mind awfully getting a jam for me, I'm all **allergic** to the back of shops, I've been **tested and everything**,' Spangles said, half remembering a medical drama he'd seen on TV recently.

Frankie rolled her eyes and went for the jam.

As soon as her back was turned, Spangles leaned through to the window display, grabbed the biggest jar of **MARBLES**, and ran.

Sausage-face Pete was mostly a fisherman, sometimes a foolish man but never a superman. He had, however, seen plenty of Superman movies and had always dreamed of getting 'changed' in a phone box. But he realised as he walked along the promenade, the slight problem with his dream was the lack of phone boxes in the modern times.

'Flippin' modern times,' he grumbled to himself and slipped into the public toilets instead. Locking himself in a cubicle, he popped the lid off the paint and proceeded to slap the blackness all over his yellowness.

Having transformed his once-bright yellow wellies, mac and hat to black, he wiggled himself in front of a hand dryer to give the quick-drying paint a helping blast of hot air, then swapped his detachable black beard for the new bright blue busher. Admiring his handiwork in the bathroom mirror, he took a stick of white chalk from his pocket and carefully drew a skull and crossbones on his hat, completing his pirate disguise. 'Aharrr!' he exclaimed to his reflection merrily, 'Ooo's a pretty boy, then?'

The aroma left in Bitterly Library by the farting intruder was hard to ignore. Freddie Taylor was researching his school homework at the time of the trumping and decided to leave.

Homework in the holidays was not exactly his idea of fun, and despite the presence of the actual for-real Smugglers' Cove in Bitterly Bay, his pirate project was looking a little ordinary. He had arranged to interview a friend of Mayor Jackson the following morning which he hoped would liven it up a bit. After all, the Mayor's friend *did* claim to be an ancestor of the legendary **Pirate Bonehead** himself.

Freddie stepped out into the early evening

sunshine, wondering if the library trumper had actually been Spangles McNasty, but decided it was probably just a coincidence. Spangles' infamous library-farting antics had started a bit of a craze in the town.

There was a notice board outside displaying a large 'No Trumping' poster that made Freddie laugh every time he saw it. You had to give Mayor Jackson credit for trying. He really did love Bitterly Bay. *The best seaside town ever!* the poster boasted, next to a little photo of the smiling Mayor in his straw beach hat and flip-flops.

To the right of the 'No Trumping' poster was an advert for the **'Diamond Skull Pirate Exhibition'** which opened on Saturday: Freddie knew it was Mayor Jackson's pride and joy. And next to that, there was a poster for the 'Best Beach Award' judges' visit on Sunday, complete with prizes for the best **pirate** fancy dress. It was going to be a busy weekend in Bitterly Bay.

The Diamond Skull

Mayor Jackson was so happy, he was skipping like a rope around the centrepiece of his new exhibition in Bitterly Museum. The two security guards he had hired specially to protect the main exhibit watched him in silence.

The younger of the pair, Sergeant Pickles, stood stiffly to attention, soldier-like, although she was neither a soldier, a sergeant or a pickle.

Her partner in security, Captain Crumples, had suggested adding the Sergeant bit to her name for business purposes.

'In the security business, people like to feel secure,' was exactly what Captain Crumples had said. Sergeant Pickles always remembered exactly what was said and always wrote it down in her daily work diary. And then spell checked it. And then filed it away alphabetically.

Captain Crumples did not do any of this. He was mostly asleep. Even when he was working. Even when he was talking he looked and sounded like he was sleeping. Which is exactly how he looked as he watched the Mayor skip around the tall plinth with the glass domed top.

Captain Crumples roused himself and checked

his watch: 8 p.m. It was going to be a long night of guarding other people's expensive nonsense – well, for Sergeant Pickles, he thought to himself. He was already looking forward to a night of sofa-snoozing,

telly-watching,

biscuit-nibbling,

milkshake-slurping athletics. Captain Crumples liked to think of his various relaxing hobbies as athletics and often wondered why they weren't in the Olympics.

'I can't thank you enough,' Mayor Jackson said, as he stopped skipping, and put his bowler hat of importance back on top of his mayoring head. He was about to give the glass dome a quick polish with his jacket sleeve when Sergeant

Pickles stopped him. 'I wouldn't do that if I were you, Mayor. The exhibit is already alarmed. If you so much as touch the glass, the alarm will start blaring.'

'Like an ice-skating camel,' Captain Crumples added sleepily.

Mayor Jackson frowned at the older, rounder security guard who was bulging out of his uniform.

A uniform that had not seen a washing machine or an iron for some time. The Mayor wondered if pretending to be asleep was part of his security guard act and was about to ask when **Professor Bonehead Junior Junior** interrupted.

The Professor clomped across the wooden floor in his knee-length **pirate-style boots** and matching knee-length **pirate-style jacket**.

'AHARRR!' he said.

It sounded a little too piratey for the modern times, but matched his **plaited ponytail** and **twirly moustache** perfectly.

'**Spangly, isn't it?**' he said grinning at the plinth displaying his precious treasure.

The mere sound of the word 'spangly' was enough to give Mayor Jackson a sudden nerve tingling fizz of the heebie-jeebies, or was it the hoo-ba-jar-bees? The filing cabinets of his memory quickly assembled and presented a slide show of a certain **Spangles McNasty** and his ridiculous friend **Sausage-face Pete** from their previous encounters.

'Are you quite all right, Mayor?' **Professor Bonehead Junior Junior** asked. 'You seem a little tense.'

The Mayor turned his attention to Captain Crumples. 'Still no sign of them?'

'Of who?' Crumples replied unhelpfully.

'No, Mayor,' Sergeant Pickles put in brightly. 'Captain Crumples here has searched the town every day for the last week. There's no sign of **Spangles McNasty** or **Sausage-face Pete**. Nor Spangles' camper van or Sausage-face Pete's boat.'

In actual fact, Captain Crumples' searches had only ever taken him as far as Shakey's Shakin' Shake Shack, next door to the museum, where he practised his milkshake-slurping athletics for an hour before returning and reporting his findings, or lack of them.

'Perhaps I should take a look around?' Pickles added eagerly, suspecting correctly that Crumples'

28

efforts were not exactly exhaustive. She flicked through her notebook to the descriptions given to her by Captain Crumples. 'Spangles McNasty is tall and skinny like a lamppost, but a lamppost in a pin-stripe suit, with a handlebar moustache and a pair of dancing caterpillar eyebrows. Sausage is shorter and rounder and yellower.

They certainly sound very **distinctive**, Mayor,' Pickles said. 'If they're out there, I'm sure I can find them.'

'I don't think that will be necessary, Sergeant Pickles,' **Professor Bonehead Junior Junior** said **confidently**. 'Really, Mayor, there's no need to worry. Captain Crumples and Sergeant Pickles here are a **superb** security team, they come **highly** recommended.'

This unexpected praise made Sergeant Pickles stand even straighter to attention and Captain Crumples crumple even further, wishing he'd never got into the security business in the first place and done something more exciting instead. In fact he decided, there and then, that this would be his last security job. Then he'd run away and join the accountants.

'I'm sure they are, Professor, but you don't know Spangles McNasty and Sausage-face Pete like I do. They are nuts. Proper nutters.'

The Professor raised an eyebrow at this unusual talk from the normally formal Mayor. Something about this pair of thieves had certainly ruffled his feathers. He had no real feathers to really ruffle in reality, of course, being a Mayor and not a bird or a fancy duster on a stick.

The Mayor stared off into the distance, his eyes seeming to focus on something, or someone, that wasn't there at all.

'Spangles McNasty has a heart as cold as an iceberg's bottom and a head that's all bald on the outside and bad on the inside, like a very rotten egg,' he said with a slight tremor to his voice.

Pickles un-flipped her notes once more. 'Yes, Mayor, my initial research concludes his top five favourite nasty habits are: shouting at babies, pulling faces at old ladies, eating cold chips from bins, farting in the library and worst of all, stealing spangly things. Or shiny, sparkly, glittery things, to be more precise.'

Captain Crumples rolled his eyes at his young partner's keenness.

'And the only reported theft recently was of two hundred not-especially spangly spades from a garden centre down the coast in Sandylands. Which doesn't sound like the work of Mr McNasty,' Sergeant Pickles concluded swiftly.

'No, I suppose not, but we can't be too careful, Sergeant, the **Diamond Skull** is an extraordinarily valuable piece,' the Mayor replied, pointing to his prize exhibit: a priceless **pirate hat** which had a **diamond-encrusted skull and crossbones** on the front.

'The skull there on the front is made with a hundred and fourteen diamonds. Not to mention the significance of this hat's place in **pirating history**, on the head of our very own Professor's great-great-great-great-great-great-great-great grandfather, **Pirate Bonehead** himself.'

The diamonds were indeed worth a fortune. The rest of the **pirate exhibition** was fantastic too, but persuading the Professor to let Bitterly Museum exhibit the **Diamond Skull** was quite possibly Mayor Jackson's finest hour.

Tourists had been flooding into town all week in their fancy-dress **pirate costumes**, eagerly anticipating the exhibition opening on Saturday morning. What with that and the Best Beach Award judges arriving on Sunday, it was shaping up to be the best weekend in Bitterly Bay's history of holidaying. If Bitterly Beach won the award, and it was looking almost certain to do so, especially with the midnightly smoothing operators he'd employed to comb the sand, it would quite probably make Mayor Jackson the most successful Mayor ever, and he liked the sound of that.

Maybe there would be a prize for such an achievement or even a statue of himself on the promenade.

Seeing the Mayor was still frowning, lost in thought, **Professor Bonehead Junior Junior** calmly lifted his right arm, extended his little pinky finger and gently touched the glass dome covering the museum's prize exhibit.

The museum's alarm immediately began wailing. 'You see, gentlemen, there really is nothing to worry about,' the Professor said calmly and walked away to turn off the alarm.

Pirate Parrot Jeff

The sun was tired after a long day's shining all over its favourite little town on the planet of Earth. It was looking forward to having the night off as it slid slowly towards the horizon. One last blast on the beach and the harbour and the funfair and all the funny little people dressed as **pirates**. The sun remembered the **real pirates** from the past. 'We're all from the past,' the sun would have said if it could talk, but it couldn't so it didn't.

It let its hot gaze linger a moment on Bitterly Pet Shop and sneaked a peek through the window. Inside, a man in full **pirate costume** (complete with blue beard) was **arguing** with the shopkeeper about a parrot.

'It's about this parrot,' the man said.

'Ah yes, the Norwegian Red,' the shopkeeper replied, admiring the colourful bird he had just sold to the man.

'It's dead,' the man said.

The shopkeeper sighed and looked at the bird.

The bird was standing on the man's shoulder in the traditional **pirate parrot position**. It **swivelled** its head to look at the man and then at the shopkeeper.

'Say something, Jeff,' the shopkeeper said.

'My name's not Jeff!' the man shouted. He was about to tell the shopkeeper his name was Sausage-face Pete when he remembered the whole point of being all disguised-up and secret.

'No, sir, that's Jeff on your shoulder. He's **normally** very talkative. Aren't you, Jeff?'

Jeff said nothing. Instead he **shuffled** his tiny **parrot feet** from side to side which didn't mean yes or no in any language, human, parrot, pirate or otherwise, but was enough to satisfy Sausage that his new **pet pirate parrot** was indeed **alive**. '**Whatever**,' he said rather **rudely** and left the shop.

The shopkeeper, known to his friends and his pets as Jimmy the Pet Shop Guy, locked the door behind him and sighed again. The excitement caused by the **pirate exhibition** was good for business, especially the parrot business, but he didn't usually stay open this late and was already looking forward to the pet shop returning to normal when the exhibition was over. '**Pesky pirates**,' he complained.

'Pesky pirates, pesky pirates!'  the ten remaining Norwegian Reds repeated together.

'Who rattled your cages, Jeffs?' Jimmy the Pet Shop Guy said. He called all of his parrots Jeff, it kept things simple. All the dogs were Dave, the snakes were all Mildred, and the hamsters all Tyson.

Sausage marched along the promenade towards the museum. 'Right then, Jeff, you know what to do,' he said. Jeff said nothing as he had no idea what Sausage was talking about.

When he reached the museum the lights were on inside but the doors locked, just as Spangles had said they would be. He knocked firmly on the door.

Inside the museum, Mayor Jackson was still admiring the **Diamond Skull** and dreaming of statues of himself for his tourism-raising antics when he heard the knock. 'Send them away, Captain, whoever they are. But be polite about it of course,' he instructed.

Captain Crumples huffed his way out of the main hall and past the reception area to the museum's front door. Putting on his best fake smile, he unlocked the heavy door and heaved it open. 'Good evening, I'm afraid we're closed. The exhibition opens at ten o'clock tomorrow morning, sir,' he said as politely and professionally as he could to the man who had knocked. Crumples noticed the man seemed to have painted his clothes black and was gripping something feathery in his right hand.

'Oh dear, Jeff – Jeff! Come back, you silly bird!' the knocker said and then threw the feathery thing in his hand over Captain Crumples' head into the museum.

Jeff had never been thrown into a museum before. He decided to make the most of it and went for a quick flap about. Captain Crumples' mental athletics were even worse than his physicals. Before he had time to think, the pirate man had barged past him and was running into the main hall after his parrot, although even Crumples noticed the parrot hadn't actually gone into the hall and was busy circling the large oval reception desk.

Sausage-face Pete headed straight for the Mayor and the main exhibit directly behind him, shouting, 'Jeff! Jeff! Come back, you naughty parrot.'

Sergeant Pickles leaped into action and also onto the pirate invader. 'Hold it right there!' she said, grabbing Sausage firmly by both shoulders.

Mayor Jackson noticed Pickles somehow already had a pair of handcuffs open and ready in each hand.

'I'm ever so sorry about Jeff, Mayor – it *is* Mayor Jackson, isn't it? I'm your biggest fan, you know. You are an amazing Mayor, bringing this exhibition to Bitterly Bay. Simply amazing.'

'Thank you, but really, there's no need, I'm only doing my job after all.' Mayor Jackson smiled his mayoral smile. 'Sergeant, I think we can let our new friend go now. You weren't about to steal the Diamond Skull, were you, sir? Ah-ha-ha-ha.' The Mayor laughed his mayoral laugh.

Sausage joined him with his own fake laugh as Pickles reluctantly let go of her first ever invader.

'Oh, I say, is that the famous hat?' Sausage

gasped at the **Diamond Skull** in its protective case
behind the Mayor.

'We're closed,' Sergeant Pickles barked
irritably, resisting the urge to drag the **pirate
invader** swiftly to the door and throw him out.
'And don't touch the glass, it's alarmed.'

'Now, now, Sergeant, the hat's quite safe, isn't
it, Mr . . .' Mayor Jackson extended a handshake
of politeness towards a suddenly panicking
Sausage-face Pete who hadn't thought he'd need
a fake name for this part of the plan. Spangles
hadn't mentioned anything
about fake
names.

'**Absolutely**, Mayor, of course, quite safe . . .' he said, stalling. '**And please call me** . . . **Jeff,**' he said at last, shaking the Mayor's hand.

'Oh. You *and* the parrot?' the Mayor said. 'Lovely,' he added, smiling his mayoral smile again.

'Your parrot, sir.' Captain Crumples placed Jeff the parrot on Jeff the pirate's shoulder as he joined them in the main hall. Jeff the parrot had quickly tired of **flapping** and had landed on Captain Crumples' head for a laugh. Captain Crumples, not finding this quite as amusing as Jeff did, was now very keen to get the **loopy** man and his **annoying** bird out of the museum and head home for some seriously relaxing athletics.

'Oh, **Jeff**, who's a **naughty boy**?' Sausage said. Everyone waited quietly for Jeff to reply, but

Jeff said nothing. 'They promised he would talk,' Sausage said, feeling genuinely short-changed with his **pet-shop pirate parrot purchase**.

'Right then, off you pop,' Crumples huffed, gesturing towards the exit sign above the door.

'**Mayor**, could I be a tiny bit of a **nuisance** before I go? May I get a **quick selfie** with you?' Sausage already had his phone in his hand and was shuffling into position next to the Mayor.

'Of course, of course, no problem at all.' Mayor Jackson pulled out his best election-winning-vote-for-me smile as Sausage clicked away, making sure he got a clear shot of the **Diamond Skull** in its alarmed display case in the background.

Suddenly, as quickly as he had burst in, Sausage-face Pete span on a squeaky wellie-booted heel and ran out of the museum, shouting over his shoulder as he went. 'Thank youooooo!'

Jeff flapped after his new owner.

'Don't forget Jeff, Jeff!' the Mayor called after the strange visitor as he and his parrot disappeared into the warm Bitterly night.

'Well, there's nothing more we can do here tonight,' **Professor Bonehead Junior Junior** said, strolling back into the main hall after one last look over the exhibits. 'Your **pirate exhibition extravaganza** is ready, Mayor.'

'There's only one thing that worries me,' Mayor Jackson said, leading the way to the exit. Sergeant Pickles locked the museum doors behind them and Captain Crumples trudged down the steps. 'Where there's treasure, Spangles McNasty will never be far away.'

'Relax, Mayor Jackson. Tomorrow will be

a momentous day for Bitterly Bay.' **Professor Bonehead** waved goodnight, leaving Mayor Jackson alone on the museum steps looking over his favourite place in the world.

It really did look like things were going his way for a change.

He watched the happy holiday-makers enjoying the end of a long sunny day. From the little harbour, all the way along the promenade, past the Town Hall, down to the funfair on the pier, everywhere he looked, Mayor Jackson saw happy smiling faces. The one face he wanted to see but actually didn't really, was missing.

'Where is he?' Mayor Jackson asked the sun-setting horizon. 'Where is that nutter and his ridiculous friend?'

All That Glitters

Sausage-face Pete slipped unnoticed through the sea of fancily dressed **piratey tourists** into Bitterly Harbour and aboard his boat which was also in disguise, pretending to be a **pirate ship**, with fake sails, a crow's-nest and a big flappy black flag with a skull and crossbones and the words **Jolly Naughty** painted beneath.

Sausage bounced over the newly installed

extra-wide boarding ramp and knocked on the shed door.

It had been Spangles' idea to hide his rusty old camper van on deck inside a large garden shed he'd made from bits of wood he'd stolen from other people's garden sheds. When he heard the knocking he put down his hammer, climbed out of the camper and approached the locked shed door.

'What did the **parrot** say to the **pirate**?' he asked.

'Who's a fluffy bumface?!' Sausage answered with the correct secret codewords. Spangles let his fishy accomplice in and quickly closed the door again, hiding his hammering from any unwanted snooping.

'Did you get it?' he asked.

'It's a *he* actually, an' he's called **Jeff**, me old name check,' Sausage answered.

'Who is?'

'Say somethin', Jeff,' Sausage instructed his new feathered friend hopefully.

'My name ain't Jeff, Sausage, you had a bump on the head or summit?'

Jeff said nothing but decided to have a look at his new home and flapped from Sausage's shoulder into the camper van, flew one quick lap around the cramped living area and landed on a spade handle. There were plenty to choose from: he counted two hundred.

'That's Jeff,' Sausage pointed to his perched parrot, as they climbed into the van.

'You weren't **supposed** to keep him, Sausage, he were just to get you in the **museum**, weren't he,' Spangles growled. 'Just keep him **away** from me creation.' He sat back down at a small table containing a half empty jar of **MARBLES**, a hammer, a pile of smashed marble pieces, two tubes of glue, a glitter gun and an almost completed fake **Diamond Skull pirate hat.**

'What d'ya reckon?' Spangles held up the hat grinning the grin of the soon-to-be rich.

Sausage never ceased to be amazed by Spangles' arts and crafts skills. For someone who claimed to hate everything, he was uncannily handy with a glitter gun.

'Would you look at the spangles on that!' Spangles added proudly. While Sausage had been pursuing pictures with the parrot part of the plan, Spangles had been busy with his hammer, glueing tiny pieces of smashed-up MARBLES to his fake Diamond Skull hat. He was very fussy about the size and shape of the pieces – they had to look enough like real diamonds to fool people under pretty close scrutiny, at least for a little while.

'Well, flip to the flop,' Sausage said, genuinely

impressed, giving the fake **Diamond Skull** a good close-up stare. After a moment he said, 'You **missed** a bit,' and pointed to a tiny gap on the skull image's chin.

'Ain't quite finished yet, just five more bits to glue on,' Spangles replied defensively, snatching the hat back. '**Anyway**, did you get the **photo**?'

'Take a **looky** see, me old **snap shot**,' Sausage said, tossing his phone to Spangles.

Spangles quickly found the photo of the museum and zoomed in to enlarge the background behind Sausage and Mayor Jackson. There it was, as plain as a sausage on a face: **the real Diamond Skull**.

Although the two naughties knew exactly what the legendary **pirate hat** looked like, after much trumping research in Bitterly Library, they hadn't known how it would be displayed in the museum. But now they did.

'That dome thing over it is all alarmed-up, too,' Sausage added, with the wisdom of a tourist information centre. 'There's a **DO NOT TOUCH** sign and everything.'

'So **all we need** now is something that looks a bit like an **old fishbowl** . . .' Spangles said, staring at the picture and giving his moustache a quick twirl for thinking effect.

'**Trevor!**' Sausage shouted suddenly.

'My name ain't Trevor either, Sausage, what you on about?'

'Didn't you used to 'ave a **fishy called Trevor** though, in them other times?'

In the corridors of Spangles' mind, a framed photo of a goldfish fell from the wall and smashed on the carpet. He had indeed once owned a fish called Trevor, who he **flushed** down a public toilet on Bitterly Promenade for a **laugh**.

Spangles quickly rummaged in a cupboard under the TV and pulled out his old fishbowl.

'Perfectio!' he said, congratulating himself with a made-up word as he tried it for size over the fake hat.

'Just print them treasure maps we drew off me laptop, there, Sausage, while I finishes me creation, then we'll be all set for our little night-time **shenanigans**.'

Pickles paced. She paced and she watched and she listened. She would rather have been hiding, pouncing and wrestling, but the pacing, watching and listening was a good warm up to the main event in the morning when she sincerely hoped someone would try to steal the **Diamond Skull**.

'The calm before the storm, as they say,' Pickles told herself, glancing briefly through a window at Bitterly Harbour as she marched past. The harbour was deserted and dead calm, much like the museum. Checking her watch as she marched into her two-hundred-and-thirty-second lap of the room, Pickles noted it was three o'clock in the morning. 'Not long now,' she said excitedly to the **Diamond Skull**, picking up the pace as she marched away from the harbour view.

Unseen and unheard in the harbour, a door opened quietly. The door belonged to a large garden shed that was not even in a garden but aboard a fishing boat all disguised-up as a **pirate ship**.

If Sergeant Pickles had lingered a little longer at the window, she would have seen a rusty old camper van emerge from the shed, coughing thick clouds of unspeakable filth from its rusty exhaust as it rolled over a wide boarding plank onto the harbour. It sped away into the deserted middle of the night and the middle of the town.

Parking discreetly between two overflowing skips, Spangles and Sausage hopped from the camper and unloaded their naughty cargo of posters and buckets of glue. 'RE-PEELABLE STICKY STUFF, THE GLUE FOR YOU', the tin boasted in tall shouty capitals.

Spangles handed Sausage half of the small posters, one of the buckets of glue and a brush, and took the rest himself. 'Right then, let's get this lot stuck up quick sharp! You do that side of town, I'll do this 'un, meet me back 'ere quick as you can,' Spangles explained, clicking the door closed as quietly as he could. 'And if anyone asks what you're doin', remember; glue 'em and run.'

'Glue 'em and run. Got it,' Sausage repeated, smiling to himself as he imagined chucking the pot of glue over a nosy parker.

Every town in the world has a nosy parker, someone who just has to know everybody else's business. They don't often have a name that rhymes with their hobby, but in Bitterly Bay there is an exceptionally nosy lady by the name of Rosie Barker the Nosy Parker. When Rosie couldn't sleep, she clopped around Bitterly Bay on her horse, Rocking.

Rocking was a real horse with a toy name. A toy name and a nosy owner who often woke him up in the middle of the night to go out 'for a nose-about', as Rosie liked to say, so she did.

'Wake up, Rocking, time for a nose-about!' she yelled at the unlucky horse who was fast asleep on the sofa in her lounge, as Rosie didn't have a stable or a garden because she lived in a flat. Luckily she lived on the ground floor, so Rocking only had to use the stairs if he wanted to go out on the roof to watch the sun set over Bitterly Bay which he did most weekends, though he preferred to use the lift.

Rocking did a big old horsey yawn as he

clopped out of the front door into a familiar quiet, night-time scene. He was not remotely interested in other peoples' business, or even other horses' business. Rocking just wanted to get the night-time nose-about over with as quickly as possible and get back to his sofa. He turned left at the end of the street and headed towards the town centre.

Sausage-face Pete was covered in glue. The 'creeping around, sticking posters up in the middle of the night' business was harder than he'd expected. He had glued twelve posters to walls, windows and lampposts and seventeen to himself, when he saw the horse approaching.

'Excuse me, young lady, what are you doing?' Rosie Barker the Nosy Parker asked as she and Rocking clopped closer.

Sausage-face Pete looked up and down the deserted street and stroked his fake beard. 'Who you callin' a lady, then?' he replied, insulted and momentarily forgetting his 'glue 'em and run' instructions.

'Oh I am sorry, sir. I forgot my spectacles,' Rosie apologised and waited for a further explanation to satisfy her nosing about.

Sausage looked up at the old lady in her dressing gown and slippers, sitting on her horse. 'Some people are sooo weird,' he said quietly to the horse.

Looking at the fake-beard-wearing, fish-stinking, middle-of-the-night-poster-sticking man covered in black paint, glue and posters, Rocking nodded his horsey head in agreement.

Sausage put his brush and the remaining posters on the ground and adjusted his grip on the bucket of glue, ready to take evasive action.

'I haven't got all night, young lady,' Rosie said impatiently (her memory was almost as bad as her eyesight). 'The sun will be up in a minute.'

Sausage peeled one of the posters from his mac and slapped it onto the side of the horse. Rocking loved his horsey clopping hooves but they weren't great for the fiddlier things in life, such as turning the pages of his morning newspaper or unsticking unwanted posters from himself. He glared at the strange man and stamped a couple of hooves quickly on the road.

If Sausage or Rosie had understood Morse code (or Horse code as Rocking preferred to call it) they would have known the stamping sounds spelled out the message, 'I am going to poop in your bed, stinky fishman.'

'Oh, stickers, is it? I see. What are they for?'

Rosie reached down and unpeeled the poster for a closer look.

It looked like this:

Wanna be all rich 'n' happy times, yay?! Just for the LOLs, Bitterly Bay Council done buried loads of bags of money all in the beach, easy as peasy to find with this 'ere map.

If only you had a spade, yeah?! Guess what?! FREE spades all over the beach this morning! Get digging! Love 'n' hugs, Mayor Jackson

Sausage held his breath and his bucket, realising his mistake. No one was supposed to see the posters until the following morning.

Luckily for Sausage-face Pete, without her glasses, Rosie only saw a blurry picture of her favourite Mayor. 'Oh, that's lovely, dear,' Rosie said, squinting at the **piratey** poster. 'Is it for the Mayor's **Pirate Exhibition** tomorrow? You better get a move on, it's almost tomorrow today,' she added confusingly.

Sausage checked his watch, the strange lady was right, the sun would be up in half an hour. Spangles would be waiting in the camper van already.

Glue 'em and run, Sausage's panicking brain reminded him.

'Would you like some help, dear?' Rosie offered, slapping the poster onto a nearby lamppost. 'Pass me the bucket.'

Sausage was about to hurl the bucket of glue over the nosy lady, but stopped himself just in time and handed it to her instead.

'I don't sleep well, you see, dear. Do I, Rocking?' Rosie said, half to Sausage and half to her horse. 'It'll give me something to do and I always like to do my bit for Bitterly Bay. Don't I, Rocking?'

'You ain't rocking, missus,' Sausage reassured the strange lady.

'Not me, dear. He's Rocking.' Rosie patted her horse who was standing perfectly still.

Sausage watched the horse for a moment. 'Nope, he ain't rocking either, missus. You been on

73

the sherry?' he asked, handing over the remaining posters.

Rosie wasn't listening, she was already engrossed in doing her bit for Bitterly Bay, slapping glue all over a shop window.

'Righty-ho then,' Sausage shouted, as he ran away. 'Thanks again!'

Sausage unpeeled the remaining sixteen posters from his mac as he ran and stuck them onto the shop windows he passed. When he arrived panting back at the camper van, he found Spangles waiting with the engine running, drumming his fingers impatiently on the steering wheel.

As soon as Sausage was aboard, the van sped away to Bitterly Beach.

'No time to lose, Sausage,' Spangles said, bouncing the camper up the kerb, over the promenade and down the wide boat ramp onto the sandy beach. 'Hop in the back there, open the door and drop 'em out while I keeps 'er movin'.'

The van zigzagged from one end of Bitterly Beach to the other, starting by the funfair-filled pier and ending beyond the Town Hall near the little harbour directly in front of Bitterly Museum. As it moved slowly over the sand, Sausage-face Pete carefully dropped a spade every few yards until all two hundred were spread over the beach.

The sun peeked its happy self over the horizon and yawned, it could never quite get used to the early starts in the summer and was already looking forward to all the winter lie-ins and short working days ahead. The sun wasn't at all nosy, but it was very observant and it had the best seat in the house to watch the daily, but not nightly, comings and goings in Bitterly Bay.

It watched the security guard in Bitterly Museum, still pacing from the day before. She passed the museum window just too late to see the camper van disappear back inside the garden shed aboard the pretend **pirate boat** in the harbour. It saw a horse and sleeping rider slowly clopping homeward along the High Street.

A little later, when the town began to wake up, it watched as three early visitors arrived at Bitterly Museum in three separate taxis. The sun didn't need spectacles to see the tiny detail of the world below and it recognised the three visitors as Mayor Jackson, **Professor Bonehead Junior Junior** and Captain Crumples, each a little too preoccupied with their own thoughts, or sleeping, to notice the overnight appearance of hundreds of small treasure maps glued randomly to walls, windows and lampposts, or the strange change to the beach.

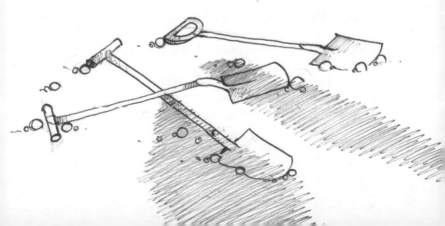

The sun noticed of course, as the newly scattered objects cast long early-morning shadows on the sand. It was looking forward to doing its bestest shining on Sunday when the Best Beach Award judges would arrive to inspect the smoothness of the Mayor's beautiful beach. It *was* a beautiful beach.

But, the sun couldn't help wondering, as it counted the two hundred spades, would it still be beautifully smooth on Sunday?

The Map in the Hat

Freddie was late. He would have normally **paddled** along the beach to get to the museum, but with all the lateness, he decided to run along the promenade instead.

He noticed a lot of new posters seemed to have appeared overnight as he ran, but didn't stop to read any. He **jogged** up the museum steps and knocked on the front door.

After a short pause the door was opened by a very excited Mayor Jackson.

'Aha! Freddie, come in come in,' beamed the Mayor. He had arranged the interview with **Professor Bonehead** as a favour to Freddie for helping out with previous problems caused by a certain Spangles McNasty.

Just thinking about the naughty spanglar gave the Mayor a sudden flush of the hee-bee-jim-blings again and he shivered as Freddie entered the museum. 'You haven't seen him, have you?' the Mayor asked. 'Or noticed anything unusual lately?'

'No, not a peep,' Freddie replied, knowing instantly what, or rather, who, the Mayor was worried about.

'Bit strange, though, don't you think? No sign of him or his ridiculous friend at all?' The Mayor began to worry all over again. He held open the door and looked over the harbour, full of jolly, dressed-up **pirate boats** with pretend crow's-nests and **pirate flags**. He noticed one of the flags read **Jolly Naughty**, which he thought was rather funny. It made him relax a little and smile.

'Now, now, Mayor, don't start all that again,' **Professor Bonehead Junior Junior** said from the main exhibition hall. 'Anything to report from last night?' he checked again with Sergeant Pickles, who hadn't stopped pacing around the room. Her thief-catching adrenaline was still racing through her veins like an Olympic hurdling rhino.

'NOTHING TO REPORT!' Pickles shouted, accidentally rather loudly, waking up Captain Crumples.

Mayor Jackson introduced Freddie to **Professor Bonehead** and the two security guards. Polite hellos were swapped, **Professor Bonehead** opting for the more unusual, **'AHARRR!'**

Sergeant Pickles eyed Freddie suspiciously, hoping he would make a sudden dash for the **Diamond Skull**.

'Nice costume,' Freddie complimented **Professor Bonehead** on his **piratey boots**, jacket and haircut.

'What costume?' the Professor replied. 'This is my everyday wear, Freddie. I could dress up if you like, though. It'd make a great cover photo for your project!'

Freddie had a sudden sinking feeling. 'Erm, well . . . it's a project about **pirates**, really, not erm—'

'AHARRR!' Professor Bonehead interrupted, lunging at Freddie suddenly, pointing a small pencil from the end of an outstretched arm. 'Ah yes, still got it,' he said happily.

'The old fencing skills, like riding a bike.'

Freddie wondered if it was too late to start a different project altogether, maybe about **deluded** exhibition curators who thought they were **pirates**.

'You've done a **fabulous** job with the exhibition, professor,' he said, trying to steer the conversation in a less mad direction.

'Oh, this was all done by my assistant, Mr Tibbs. I don't really have the time.'

'Ah, busy **researching**?' Freddie guessed.

'No, no, that's all done by Mr Tibbs, too.' Freddie waited for the explanation to continue but it didn't. Instead **Professor Bonehead** said, 'Shall we use the office? Bit quieter, shipmate!' and led the way out of the exhibition hall just as Mayor Jackson's phone rang.

'That'll be my secretary, Marjory, with the press conference details. Showtime in thirty minutes, people,' the Mayor said brightly as he answered the call.

'Mayor Jackson, thank goodness it's you!' Marjory shrieked.

'Who did you expect, Marjory?' Mayor Jackson asked, thinking for the millionth time that week that maybe it was time to get a new secretary. Marjory's behaviour just kept getting weirder and weirder.

'First things first, Marjory, how's the beach?'

This was not quite such an unusual question as it sounds because Marjory was actually on the beach, in the Mayor's beach-hut office to be precise.

Mayor Jackson had two offices, the official one in the Town Hall which was completely resplendent and totally grand, not to mention suitably posh, and a second unofficial, small, blue-and-white striped beach-hut office, sitting in a row of other brightly painted beach huts at the top of Bitterly Beach. He was so anxious about the Best Beach Award judges' forthcoming visit he'd asked Marjory to spend the night on 'Beach Watch'.

Marjory had watched the beach for a while as the holiday-makers gradually left and the sun slowly set, but it wasn't quite the thrilling undercover operation she'd hoped for. So she'd spent the rest of the night playing with a new game on her laptop. It was a spinoff of her favourite online cookery programme, SPOOKY COOKY, an almost-reality show which investigated tales of haunted food.

The game featured some of her favourite episodes, including the one with the nightmare noodles and the knitting, and the one with the haunted eggs and the hammer.

With the beach hut's door firmly shut and her duvet over her head, Marjory hadn't seen or heard anything from the beach all night.

The lack of sleep and overdose of haunting entertainment had left her all jittery and jumpy.

'Can I have a hug?' she asked.

Mayor Jackson massaged his frowning forehead as he circled the exhibition hall, falling in line behind the pacing Pickles.

He decided to change the subject. 'How about the press conference, are we all set for nine-thirty?' he tried, hoping for once there would be a simple answer and it would be 'yes'.

Marjory's concentration had drifted back to her laptop, where the tempting question PLAY AGAIN? was blinking at her from the end of her last attempt at level forty-three of the SPOOKY COOKY game. 'Lawks, why not?' she squealed with delight and hung up the phone.

Mayor Jackson stopped pacing and was about to phone Marjory back but decided he was unlikely to get a more sensible answer anyway and his time would be better spent working on his speech for the opening ceremony instead. He made himself comfortable at the large desk in the reception area.

In the museum office, Freddie sat opposite **Professor Bonehead Junior Junior** at an antique oak desk, beneath a large glass chandelier. He took out his notepad and hoped for the best. 'Professor, could you tell me a little about your ancestor, **Pirate Bonehead**?"

'He was like me in a lot of ways,' the Professor answered, leaping up from his chair and planting both fists firmly on his hips.

'He was a museum curator?' Freddie asked, confused.

'No, no, I mean we are both dashing, daring . . . swashbuckling types.'

'Erm . . . OK. I read that some historians think all of the diamonds now embedded in his famous hat 'the **Diamond Skull**' were actually given to **Pirate Bonehead** by several queens he had romanced. Rather than him stealing them in the traditional pirate manner. Do you think there's any truth in this rumour?'

'Absolutely, yes. As I say, we are very alike, my ancestor and I. It's in the genes, you know.

And it's *my* hat, by the way.' **Professor Bonehead** suddenly jumped up onto the desk in front of Freddie.

'Erm. Right,' Freddie said, pushing his chair backwards slightly.

'Would you like me to try it on for the photo?'

'Well. It's not really a project about you as such. It's about **pirates**. Speaking of which, there are also rumours that **Pirate Bonehead** had a treasure chest that he buried which has never been found. Do you think this is true?'

'I buried some treasure once!' the Professor announced. Leaping from the table, he grabbed the fancy chandelier hanging from the office ceiling and swung across the room, kicking his legs wildly.

Freddie jumped up before the Professor swang back. 'That's, erm . . . Well, that's nice. But what about **Pirate Bonehead's lost treasure**?'

The Professor let go of the chandelier, missed the table completely and landed in a tangled heap on the floor. He immediately jumped up again and said, '**Lost? Oh no**, I found it again the next day. **I'd drawn a map you see**.'

Freddie closed his notepad and decided to talk about **pirate stories** instead. 'Have you seen the movie *The Map in the Hat*?' he asked. 'That's a great **pirate film**. There's this **crazy pirate guy** who sets a trap for his archenemy by putting a fake treasure map in his hat and letting the other guy steal it . . .' Freddie suddenly stopped mid-sentence and ran out of the office to find the Mayor.

'Rude,' **Professor Bonehead Junior Junior** said to himself and turned to his computer to search for the film, as it was one of the very few **pirate movies** he'd never seen.

Freddie found the Mayor trying out his speech on Captain Crumples, who looked like he had fallen asleep standing next to the **Diamond Skull**.

'Excuse me, Captain,' Freddie said, waking the slumbering security guard. 'Have you put a tracking device in the hat? You know . . . just in case.'

'Just in case what?' Crumples grumbled sleepily.

'In case you need to track it. To find it again, if it's stolen, I mean.'

'Stolen!' Sergeant Pickles snapped, excitedly.

'That hat's not going anywhere, young man. You can try it if you like. Grab it now and see if you can make it to the door.' Sergeant Pickles crouched, ready to pounce.

'We're not like the ones off the telly, lad,' Captain Crumples explained, yawning. 'We don't do fancy tracking devices and car chases and leaping about, do we, Sergeant?'

Sergeant Pickles remained crouched like a coiled rocket, staring at Freddie.

'What if we hid something inside the hat, Mayor?' Freddie suggested. 'Something for you-know-who, just in case he somehow gets his hands on it.'

'Like a present?' Crumples asked.

'Not exactly, Captain, more like a 𝐭𝐫𝐚𝐩,' Freddie replied.

There was a knock at the door. 'That'll be the press. We don't have much time, Freddie. If you think it'll stop you-know-who, then put it in the hat, whatever it is. Sergeant Pickles, could you help Freddie here with the alarm. Now, if you'll excuse me, I have an exhibition to open.' The Mayor left the exhibition hall to organise the opening press conference.

Freddie flipped through his notepad. The best

bit of his project by far was a map he'd made of Smugglers' Cove. He'd even done the old **tea-bag staining trick** and burnt the edges a bit with a candle. He added a hastily made-up rhyme and carefully slipped it under the lining inside the **Diamond Skull hat**. He left a corner poking out for any uninvited peepers to find.

Since parking the camper van back aboard the **Jolly Naughty** and skipping excitedly down the boat's short wooden staircase into the Captain's Cabin, Spangles and Sausage had been **patiently** waiting for the museum to open. Sausage liked to call the main living area on his fishing boat the Captain's Cabin because it sounded rather fancy but in reality it was a dingy, fish-stinking room where he either sorted and packed his fishies when fishing, or watched telly when he wasn't, and he wasn't now, so he was.

Spangles pulled a long bright-red overcoat over his striped suit and turned up the very high collar to hide his distinctive moustache. He placed the completed fake **Diamond Skull hat** on his baldy head with a triumphant, **'Ta-dah!'**

'Think you means, "Aharrr! There, me old peg leg!"' Sausage said, checking his friend's **piratey disguise**.

'**Good idea**, all this disguisin' lark! We fits right in, **like bananas in a bunch**,' Spangles replied, admiring his hat in a wonky mirror.

'**Geniosity**,' Sausage said, congratulating Spangles with a made-up word of his own, hoping Jeff would repeat it.

Jeff was once again standing on Sausage's shoulder but was beginning to think leaving the pet shop had been a bad move and maybe it was time to fly home and see all the other Jeffs again.

'The museum opens in two minutes, **let's get rich**!' Spangles beamed. He added a huge, droopy blue feather to the fake hat which flopped all over the made-of-**MARBLES** fake-diamond skull emblem, hiding it completely. Then he grabbed his beach bag and gangled up the stairs.

Pirate Fever

'Ladies and gentlemen, if I could have your attention please.' Mayor Jackson beamed as he addressed the journalists in the museum's main exhibition hall.

He had never been so happy. For once, everything seemed to be going his way. He was about to open the greatest tourist attraction Bitterly Bay had ever seen, the Best Beach Award was practically in the bag, and there was still no sign of Spangles McNasty or his ridiculous Sausage-faced friend.

Freddie decided to stay for the opening of the exhibition, hoping it might liven up his project somehow. He watched as cameras flashed merrily, snapping away at the precious **Diamond Skull**, Mayor Jackson gave a triumphant speech about the complete fabulousness of Bitterly Bay, **Professor Bonehead Junior Junior** posed happily for more photos of himself with his ancestor's hat, Sergeant Pickles kept a very close eye on the throng of journalists and Captain Crumples took the opportunity to have a sneaky snooze.

As Mayor Jackson's pocket watch ticked to ten o'clock, he ushered the photographers to the museum's front door, ready to snap the huge crowd of visitors as they swarmed in.

'Is everybody ready?' Mayor Jackson shouted, with pantomime excitement. The snappers raised their cameras in anticipation of the rush,

Pickles crouched in anticipation of the theft and Crumples snored in anticipation of more snoring.

Mayor Jackson swung open the museum door wide and shouted a theatrical 'Welcome!' to the waiting world outside.

'Hello,' replied two very **pirately** dressed figures standing on the sunny steps.

The photographers lowered their cameras, Pickles stood up and relaxed, Crumples relaxed and relaxed.

Mayor Jackson stepped outside and walked around the tiny gathering. It wasn't enough for a crowd. It wasn't even enough for a queue. He looked up and down the promenade. The street was deserted. He could hear people on the beach in the distance out of sight.

His phone rang. As he answered it, he hardly noticed the two **piratey** figures walk past him into the museum. He didn't even notice the parrot called Jeff, sitting on the shoulder of the man who had introduced himself as Jeff the previous evening.

Jeff the parrot noticed the Mayor. Jeff noticed everything and was about to say something about all of the everythings he had been noticing lately, but the Mayor was suddenly very excitably busy on his phone.

'Marjory, Marjory! Slow down, for goodness' sake. Whatever is the matter?' he said, hoping for a sensible answer but expecting one on the subject of a haunted breakfast.

'It's the b-b-b-b-h-h-b—' Marjory stammered.

'Broccoli?' Mayor Jackson guessed, staring at the empty street.

'No, the s-s-s-s-s–'

'Sandwiches?'

'Sand!' Marjory shrieked at last. 'The beach!'

Mayor Jackson froze.

'They're digging up the beach, Mayor!'

'Who is, Marjory? Who is digging up the beach?' the Mayor asked fearfully, looking along the promenade towards the unseen distant digging on his precious beach.

'EVERYONE!' Marjory screamed.

'Where is everyone, Mayor?' **Professor Bonehead Junior Junior** asked, joining the Mayor on the sunny steps.

Mayor Jackson grabbed the Professor by the lapels of his **piratey** jacket and screamed,

'The beach!

They're digging up the beach, Professor!'

'Who is?' **Professor Bonehead** asked.

'EVERYONE!' the Mayor replied, turning his panic volume up to the max.

'Is everything OK, Mayor?' Sergeant Pickles asked, hoping the answer would be 'No,' and pouncing action would be required immediately.

The Mayor glanced back inside the museum at the two visitors wandering casually around the main exhibition hall. They didn't even seem particularly interested in the **Diamond Skull**. 'Captain Crumples, you stay here. If you need us, give me a ring,' he shouted back into the museum as he ran down the steps. 'Everyone else, follow me.'

The gathered press people, sensing a far more exciting story, followed the Mayor, **Professor**

Bonehead, Freddie and Sergeant Pickles along the promenade towards the beach.

Spangles McNasty **peered** through the large blue feather **drooping** across his face from his pirate hat. He watched as Sausage crept closer to the still-sleeping Captain Crumples and poked him gently. Captain Crumples continued **snoring** peacefully.

'**Right then, me old cops an' robbers,**' Sausage said, returning to admire the real **Diamond Skull**

with Spangles. 'He's **fast asleep**, but he won't **sleep through the alarm** when you **touch this 'ere display case**.' Sausage rolled out the contents of his observations like a **carpet of facts** from the **discount carpet warehouse** of his mind.

'**Flippin' Mayor** was supposed to take him to the beach. That was the **whole point** of all the **spades and posters**,' Spangles complained.

'**Leave him to me**. I know what'll keep him 'appy,' Sausage said **confidently**, and ran back outside. He ran to Shakey's Shakin' Shake Shack next door, bought a big pink milkshake and ran back.

'I seen him **slurpin' these** in Shakey's every day last week. **Watch this . . .**'

Bitterly Beach was completely covered in **pirately** dressed tourists wielding spades and little treasure map posters, all manically digging up the once-beautifully tidy golden sand and piling it in big, messy heaps. Two hundred spades dug two hundred holes every few minutes and then quickly moved a step or two away and started again.

Marjory ran from the Mayor's beach-hut office into the throng of **pirates** and grabbed the nearest spade, trying to yank it away from its owner.

'Hey! Get your own,' the pirate digger yelled, wide-eyed with treasure-seeking excitement.

'What are you doing?' Marjory demanded, refusing to let go of the spade.

'Haven't you heard? There's treasure buried all over the beach!' the pirate digger replied.

'Says who?' Marjory released the spade and folded her arms in an 'I can't believe this nonsense, it can't possibly be true' style.

'THE MAYOR!' The **pirate** digger said confidently and thrust his map at Marjory.

Marjory examined the map closely. There was a rather crude drawing of Bitterly Beach covered with a dense scattering of small X marks and a short letter beneath. She was staring, open-mouthed at the surprise ending, where the letter finished with the flourish, *'Get diggin'! Love 'n' hugs, Mayor Jackson,'* when the breathless Mayor himself arrived with the photographers, Sergeant Pickles and Freddie.

Wanna be all rich 'n' happy times, yay?! Just for the LOLs, Bitterly Bay Council done buried loads of bags of money all in the beach, easy as peasy to find with this 'ere map.

The photographers disappeared into the crowd, snapping excitedly.

Pickles immediately leaped on the nearest digger, screaming, 'Give me that spade!'

Freddie stayed with the Mayor, wondering how he could add this madness into his pirate project.

'What? What? What?!' was all the Mayor managed to say when he saw the poster, his official brainwaves flapping like a parachuting penguin without a parachute.

He ran to his beach-hut office and quickly dialled the Chief Constable of Bitterly Police.

Chief Nutter had given the Mayor his direct line for emergencies. (He had probably never expected the emergency to involve digging sand on the beach.)

'Good morning, Chief Nutter speaking,' he answered calmly.

Mayor Jackson yelled.

'MY BEEEACH!'

'Mayor Jackson?' Chief Nutter guessed.

'They're digging up my beautiful beach!'

'Who is?' Chief Nutter asked, more than a little confused by the early morning excitement in his ear.

'EVERYONE!' Mayor Jackson screamed, staring at the chaos on the beach beyond.

'Mayor Jackson, not only is digging on the beach not against the law, it is actually what the beach is for,' Chief Nutter explained. 'Well, that and keeping the sea in the sea and not on the land. You'll be asking me to arrest people for visiting your exhibition and looking at the **Diamond Skull** next, I suppose.'

Mayor Jackson dropped the phone in shock and muttered in horror, 'Oh no, the **Diamond Skull**!'

The Old Switcheroo

Captain Crumples was an expert snorer. He sometimes snored so loudly cows in a farm three miles from his house complained about the noise, although only to each other because cows can only speak cow.

He was doing some of his finest cow-complaint-level snoring as Sausage-face Pete strolled calmly past him in the museum into the next room.

He turned and waved back at his puzzled accomplice. Delving a hand deep into one of the large pockets of his once-yellow-now-black-mac, he pulled out a tiny television set and placed it on a chair before stepping out of sight, where he carefully placed the big pink milkshake on the floor and rummaged in his other pocket for a large self-inflating sofa and a packet of biscuits. Leaving the sofa by the milkshake, Sausage walked back to join Spangles, dropping biscuits as he went.

When he arrived, a bemused Spangles said simply, 'This **better** be good, Sausage. The Mayor won't be gone **much longer**.'

'Just act natural. Like you're just lookin' at the stuff.' Sausage waved his left hand vaguely at the surrounding exhibits and with his right,

fished a TV remote from his pocket, pointed it at the distant TV set and switched it on.

The familiar sound of morning television woke the slumbering Captain Crumples. Looking around the exhibition hall, he was pleased to see it was almost deserted: only two visitors to watch, and they looked pretty harmless. He was even more pleased to see a biscuit on the floor near his foot. He picked it up, popped it straight in his mouth and noticed another one nearby. Crumples followed the biscuit trail all the way to the television and comfy sofa.

When he saw the milkshake, he couldn't quite believe his luck and, without stopping to question why such lovely treats had suddenly appeared in the museum, he sat down and began dunking his collected biscuits in the milkshake and watching the TV.

Spangles' bushy eyebrows danced their approval across his forehead.

'A sailor is always prepared,' Sausage beamed.

They gathered around the **Diamond Skull** beneath its alarmed glass dome, sitting quietly on its display stand. Spangles took a hammer from his beach bag and handed it to Sausage. He then took the fishbowl from the bag and his **pirate hat** from his head. With his free hand Sausage took a dustpan and brush from his other pocket.

'When I nods me head, hit it,' Spangles said.

Sausage grinned, tempted.

Spangles nodded.

Sausage whacked the glass dome with the hammer, smashing it to pieces. He immediately dropped the hammer back into the beach bag.

The alarm wailed.

Captain Crumples almost choked on a milky biscuit.

Sausage frantically swept the broken glass from the floor and dropped it all into the beach bag.

Captain Crumples ran.

Spangles swapped the **Diamond Skull hat** on the plinth for the fake he had been wearing. He took the large blue feather from his fake hat and pinned it to the real **Diamond Skull** now on his head and popped the upturned fishbowl over the fake.

They both turned and stepped away from the fake **Diamond Skull** and fishbowl display as Captain Crumples stomped back into the room, with a milkshake in one hand and a fist full of biscuits in the other.

'Stop right there!' he panted, spitting soggy biscuit crumbs all over the floor.

Spangles McNasty and Sausage-face Pete ignored him and continued pretending to admire various exhibits around the room. **'Excuse me, sir,'** Spangles said as politely as he had ever spoken in his entire life. 'Could you do something about that awful alarm? **I have a headache**.'

'Oh . . . there must be . . . erm . . .' Captain Crumples replied, **frowning** at the **Diamond Skull** as if it were an impossible maths equation.

It was the only exhibit connected to the alarm, but it appeared to be unharmed and no one was anywhere near it. 'Did you touch the **Diamond Skull**?' he asked. 'The alarm's very sensitive . . .'

'I simply **can't bear it** any longer,' Spangles

added dramatically, 'We shall have to **leave at once**.' He stepped towards the exit with the real **Diamond Skull** spangling on top of his baldy head, its priceless skull emblem hidden behind the droopy blue feather. He could barely contain his excitement, his biggest and boldest steal ever – and he was about to get away with the treasure.

'**Smash and grab! Smash and grab!**' Jeff suddenly squawked.

Sausage froze. Spangles glared at him.

'**On his head, on his head!**' Jeff was suddenly feeling very talkative.

'**Hammers and fish! Stop the thief!**' Jeff squawked on.

Captain Crumples stepped in front of Spangles, blocking his path to the exit.

'What's up with old feathers here?' he asked.

'Oh, take no notice. **He's broken**,' Spangles answered. 'We're on our way back to the shop now, aren't we?' he **snarled** through gritted teeth at Sausage-face Pete.

'Made of marbles! Glitter and spades!' Jeff was enjoying himself enormously, nodding at the guilty parties as he explained his collected noticings.

Sausage-face Pete suddenly **grabbed** Jeff and stuffed him into one of his mac's pockets, smiling his best innocent smile at Captain Crumples as he did so.

Captain Crumples had hoped for a quiet day's **snoozy** security guarding, and was wishing he was tucked up in bed at home. Suddenly, he had an idea, quickly followed by an even better one leap-frogging the first in a race to escape the museum and the security business altogether. If the alarm was broken, which it seemed to be, and there were no visitors anyway, which there wouldn't be as soon as he'd thrown these two loons out, he could close the museum and go home. And stay there.

So he did.

The Trap in the Hat

The note stuck to the museum door did nothing to calm the Mayor's mood when he returned, still breathless, to the top of the sunny steps.

The **wailing** alarm wasn't helping either.

'What's going on?' was all he managed to say to the locked door which informed him rather bluntly:

Alarm bust.
Gone to join
the
accountants
C.C. x

Sergeant Pickles unlocked the door and removed the note with a calmness that was eluding the Mayor. Once inside, Pickles marched briskly into the main hall, where she noted, to her disappointment, the **Diamond Skull** was still perched on its plinth beneath its alarmed glass dome. **Professor Bonehead Junior Junior** saw this too and continued his own walk of briskness to the office to turn off the alarm.

Mayor Jackson paced a tight, unhappy circle around the **Diamond Skull** with a finger in each ear. 'Everything had been going so well, Freddie,' he shouted above the din. 'At least the **Diamond Skull** is safe.' He nodded towards his prize exhibit, wondering how he could get everyone off the beach and back into the museum and if he could possibly restore the beach to its former smooth, sandy glory before the Best Beach Award judges arrived on Sunday.

Freddie lifted the glass dome from the **Diamond Skull**. 'There's something very fishy about this, Mayor,' he said as he turned the glass over and examined it more closely. Freddie had a goldfish at home which he looked after very carefully, changing the water regularly, because if he didn't, the water quickly became murky and left a grimy surface line around the bowl. Just like the one on the glass bowl he was holding now.

The alarm finally stopped wailing and **Professor Bonehead** reappeared at a run, waving a handful of computer print outs. 'There's something very fishy about this, Mayor,' he said.

'The alarm report says it was triggered by the display case being smashed. But there it is?' The Professor pointed at the glass dome Freddie was holding.

'This is a fishbowl,' Freddie announced, handing the glass bowl to the Professor and picking up the hat. 'And this,' he said dramatically, 'is a fake.'

He flipped the hat over and saw that the map he'd hidden inside the real **Diamond Skull** was missing, presumably still tucked away safely where he'd left it.

Spangles McNasty could not stop grinning. He had walked out of Bitterly Museum with the priceless **Diamond Skull** on his head! Right in front of the so-called security guard with the alarm wailing away around him. And now he was sailing out of Bitterly Harbour aboard the **Jolly Naughty** with the stolen treasure *still* on his head.

This had never happened before.

Usually, it was around about this point in the collecting, when he thought he'd got away with it, he found by some cruel twist of fate that he hadn't. And, as was becoming almost traditional, he would scream his naughty head off. But not today.

Today, for once, he had actually won.

'**We only flippin' did it, Sausage!**' Spangles grinned at his sausage-faced friend. '**We flippin' floppin' well did it!**' He took the **Diamond Skull** from his baldy head and offered it to Sausage-face Pete. '**We won! Look at the spangles on that!**' He almost shouted this last bit, like a sort of catchphrase for the modern-day collector, but composed himself a little and added, '**But seriously, try it on.**'

Sausage-face Pete did not remove his oversized once-yellow-now-black fisherman's hat very often. Mostly because it was connected to his beard by elastic, so it was a bit **faffy**, not to mention bushy, but also because he preferred to remain disguised.

'**Don't touch my hat!**' he suddenly shouted

at Spangles, without taking his eyes or his concentration off his sailing, or his hat off his head.

Spangles was way too happy to get into a grump with his old friend. He turned the hat over to pop back on to his own naughty head and noticed a small corner of folded paper poking out from the lining inside.

Spangles' mind cogs were wired differently to most peoples. To Spangles, everything was potentially either a thing to scoop from a bin and eat, to shout at, to pull a face at, to fart at, or best of all, a thing to collect. And he sensed immediately this poking paper was a possible collector.

Easing the paper from the lining, he popped the spangly hat on the table and unfolded the mysterious slip.

134

A moment later, his caterpillar eyebrows almost danced right off the top of his head and went for a swim. Thrusting the unfolded mystery under Sausage's nose, he jabbered, 'Sausage! **Is this what I thinks it is?**'

'Yup. **It's a piece of paper**, is what it is. But someone already used it **so it ain't much good** no more, is it?' Sausage replied.

'**Sausage!**' Spangles grabbed his friend by the collar of his once-yellow-now-black fishing mac and pulled him nose touchingly close. '**It's a map!**'

'**It's a treasure map!**'

'Treasure?' Sausage repeated. 'You sure? Seems a little **too good to be true**, don't it? And you know what they says about that, don't you?'

'**Nope,**' Spangles replied, his eyebrows still dancing merrily at the thought of more spangly treasure to collect, 'unless they says, "Treasure's ready, come an' get it!"'

'**It can't be real,**' Sausage continued, pondering. 'The Mayor would have found it, wouldn't he, Jeff?' The parrot decided to keep quiet as he didn't fancy being stuffed in the stinky man's fishy pocket again.

'**Nah**, it was hid, see? Just **wriggled free** cos I was all **jigglin'** it about with me **dancin' eyebrows**, look!' Spangles waggled his caterpillars expertly as if somehow proving beyond all doubt the map in the hat was completely real, and not even slightly a tea-stained faker.

Sausage wasn't so sure but he also knew that once Spangles got a whiff of collecting in his mind-box, there was no stopping him. 'It's Smugglers' Cove, all right, I'd recognise that little bay anywhere,' Sausage said, examining the map with his nauticals and also his eyes.

He read aloud the instructions which appeared to have been written with a strong pirate accent:

Saily thee to Smuggler's Cove
for treasure that's the bestest!
Step ye ten from Turtle Rock
the sea be on your leftest.
Turn ye back upon the waves
and after fourteen more,
There be Pirate Bonehead's treasure
hid beneath the floor.
AHARRRR!

Sausage glared snobbishly at the awful rhyme. 'Weren't much good at the old poetry, were he?' he said and felt a song of his own coming on.

'To Smugglers' Cove, Sausage, no time to lose!' Spangles announced gleefully.

Sausage span the **Jolly Naughty**'s wheel to the right, changing course and heading north, as he launched into a new sea shanty:

Smash it and grab it and run away, hurrah!
Hurrah!
We done a good steal, for real, for real, hurrah!
Hurrah!
Now we're all rich and we're gonna get richer,
Richer than footballers on a football pitcher.
Riches not twitchers or witches in britches:
And that's old fashioned for trouuuuusers!

Smugglers' Cove

The sun beamed its happy heat down on Smugglers' Cove. To the sun it seemed like only yesterday the small sandy beach nestled in the rocky footing of the Jelly Cliffs was **bustling** with **real pirates**, loading and unloading their stolen **booty**.

The sun also remembered **fondly** when the word 'booty' used to mean stolen treasure and not 'bottom' which it seemed to these days.

It was enjoying the commotion on Bitterly Beach, with all the digging and shouting, but felt a little sorry for the Mayor and was thinking about asking the rain if it fancied taking over for a bit to chase the diggers away. But when the sun noticed two boats sailing towards Smugglers' Cove from opposite directions, it changed its mind. Things were hotting up nicely.

One boat **chugged** rather slowly from the harbour, flying a pretend **pirate flag**. The other came **speeding** out of the Coast Guard station north of the Jelly Cliffs.

Splasher Harris stood at the controls of the speeding boat, **grinning** happily into the spray as it bounced over the waves. Mayor Jackson clung on to his seat with equal amounts of **bouncing**, but considerably less grinning.

The Mayor had arranged for his limousine to collect them from the museum, dropping off Freddie and **Professor Bonehead** at the entrance to the old smuggler's tunnel which led down to Smugglers' Cove. They had left Sergeant Pickles behind to guard the rest of the exhibition. Pickles was initially **delighted** at the idea of having sole responsibility for the exhibition, until Freddie decided it might be useful to take the fake **Diamond Skull hat** with him and Mayor Jackson agreed.

Stopping someone **stealing** a fake hat would have still been fun, but now there was no hat at all to steal and still no visitors to steal it. Sergeant Pickles soon gave up **pacing** around the deserted, hatless exhibition and plonked herself down in front of the TV on the inflatable sofa instead.

As they drove away from the museum, Freddie explained his plan. Spangles and Sausage would be unable to resist the lure of more treasure and sail to Smugglers' Cove, where they would be trapped between himself and **Professor Bonehead** hiding in the old smugglers' tunnel and Mayor Jackson, approaching from the sea with Splasher Harris.

Freddie was pleased his **piratey** research had come in handy. The tunnel was still passable all the way from its entrance near Trifle Ridge, through to Smugglers' Cove, although the entrance at either end was now sealed with a heavy iron gate because of the 'Health and Safety palaver', as Mayor Jackson called it.

Using the Mayor's keys, he hurriedly unlocked the gate at Trifle Ridge and heaved it

143

open. Its rusty hinges squeaked like evil mice.

'Yo-ho-ho, me hearties! You should have seen it back in the day, Freddie!' **Professor Bonehead** shouted and ran into the echoey tunnel. 'Shiver me timbers! Blunderbusses and beards and cussin' everywhere!'

Freddie closed the gate behind him and ran after the Professor, holding onto the fake **Diamond Skull hat** he was now wearing. 'You mean three hundred years before you were born?' he said, noticing that for someone who had just lost his priceless hat, the Professor seemed to be enjoying himself far too much.

'Well, yes. But can you just imagine?!'

The tunnel emerged at the back of a dark cave in Smugglers' Cove. Freddie fumbled with the keys at the second gate, while the Professor disappeared briefly into the shadows of the cave and reappeared dragging a cannon, yelling, 'AHARRR, me hearties!'

'Keep quiet, Professor, we're supposed to be hiding!' Freddie hushed, losing his patience. He finally got the gate open. 'What on earth is that?' he said, watching as the Professor dragged the cannon out onto the beach.

'Avast, me lad, 'tis a cannon!' **Professor Bonehead Junior Junior** replied, grinning madly.

'I can see that, but what is it doing here?'

''Tis a fully restored seventeenth-century gun, taken from the deck of the sunken *Black Dog*, captained by Mad Dog Barista himself. **AHARRR!**' The Professor pulled the cannon down to the middle of the deserted cove and pointed it out to sea.

'Captain Barista?' Freddie asked, doubtfully.

'**Yes, lad!** Terror of the high seas when I was a boy!' **Professor Bonehead** growled back, all buccaneer and plunder.

'When you were a boy . . . in the nineteen-eighties?' Freddie replied.

Professor Bonehead ran back to join Freddie in the shadows of the cave. '**Erm . . . well**, you know. I read about him **when I was a boy**, was what I meant,' he said, awkwardly, calming down a little. '**Anyway**, I had my assistant Mr Tibbs bring the cannon to the tunnel so I can give the Mayor a one-gun salute on Sunday when he wins the Best Beach Award, you see,' he explained.

'If he wins, you mean,' Freddie said, remembering the current state of Bitterly Beach and its excitable treasure-seekers.

'Makes a fine decoration, though, don't you think? To help entice our thieves onto the beach?'

Freddie didn't think it could do any harm, so didn't argue any more. They crept back further into the shadows.

Freddie tripped on a boulder, and landed on several others. He noticed they were all unusually smooth.

'**AHARRR!** See you found my cannonballs,' **Professor Bonehead** said. 'Mr Tibbs left a few extra, for practice.'

Freddie fumbled in the darkness for the fake **Diamond Skull** which had slipped from his head when he fell. When he finally found it, he stuffed it under his T-shirt instead for safe-keeping.

'Pity we didn't keep any of them spades,' Spangles said as the **Jolly Naughty** chugged closer to Smugglers' Cove, **'buried treasure is usually buried after all**. Don't suppose you've got a couple in them always prepared pockets of yours?'

'Don't be daft, me old sandcastle, they wouldn't fit. I've got a couple down below, though.' Sausage grinned.

Spangles peered greedily through a borrowed telescope. **'Treasure ahoy!'** he shouted, all flick flacks and happy times when he spotted the cannon on the beach.

Sausage snatched his telescope back and

checked for himself. 'You do know **that's a cannon**, don't you, **me old eye test?**'

'Sure is, and you know the old sayin', don't you, Sausage: **"Where there's cannons, there's treasure!"**'

'Think it's more, **"Where there's smokin', there's coughin"** or summit. Or is it smokin' and coffins?' Sausage mumbled, lost in thought, which was an occupational **hazard** for him. Every time he thought about anything, he got lost.

'Smokin' in coffins, smokin' in coffins,' Jeff remarked from Sausage's shoulder, without realising the **weirdness** of his wisdom.

The **Jolly Naughty** chugged into the bay. Sausage-face Pete moored it expertly by Turtle Rock, which was indeed totally turtle-shaped. The real **Diamond Skull** spangled magnificently on Spangles' head as he and Sausage hopped ashore, carrying a spade each and **Pirate Bonehead's** treasure map.

'**Step ye ten from Turtle Rock, the sea be on your leftest,**' Sausage read out the awful rhyming instructions again. He looked around for a clue and then began striding up the beach, straight at the tunnel where Freddie and **Professor Bonehead** were hiding.

Spangles shook his head in wonder at his friend's bottomless lack of brains or brain full of bottoms or whatever the problem was.

'Sausage!' he shouted, 'This way's left!'

'It's more a question of how many is left, me old abacus . . .' Sausage began to explain before seeing Spangles striding off purposefully in a completely different direction. Sausage ran to join him. 'And then erm . . . Turn ye back upon the waves and after fourteen more, there be Captain Bonehead's treasure hid beneath the floor.' He harrumphed his dislike of the rhyme one last time, then they counted fourteen steps and got busy digging.

Mayor Jackson and Splasher Harris sped round the headland and spotted the thieves digging on the beach as they'd hoped. Mayor Jackson almost laughed with delight when he saw Spangles was still wearing the real **Diamond Skull hat**. 'Full speed ahead, Mr Harris!' he growled. 'They won't get away with it this time.'

Meanwhile, Freddie was still crouching in the tunnel watching the two naughties as they paced around the beach with the fake map and started digging. 'Professor, do you think we should . . . Professor?' Freddie looked around in the gloom but **Professor Bonehead** was nowhere to be seen.

'Just like climbing the rigging to the crow's-nest, matey!'

Freddie looked up and saw the Professor clinging onto the rocky tunnel walls about twenty-feet off the ground. 'Will you get down here and help!' Freddie hissed.

Out at sea he saw the Coast Guard boat shoot round the headland from the north and turn towards the beach. Freddie decided to take matters, and hats, into his own hands and darted out of the cave towards Spangles and Sausage-face Pete who were busy digging as merrily as they were singing.

Sausage was singing a particularly sweary sea shanty he saved for special occasions such as this and was enjoying himself enormously. In fact, every single word in the song was a swearer, so it's probably best not to repeat it here.

The sun looked down on this peculiar scene and suddenly wished it had fingers to stick in its ears and also ears to stick the fingers in. It hadn't heard such language since the dinosaur times when Terry the T. Rex saw that asteroid.

Spangles and Sausage were so engrossed in

their digging, they didn't see Freddie until it was too late. Freddie timed his run-up perfectly to avoid the swinging spades. He leaped at Spangles and snatched the **Diamond Skull** from his baldy bonce so swiftly the floppy blue feather didn't know what had happened and was left floating, floopily behind.

'My treasure!' Spangles yelled.

'Where?' Sausage asked, knee-deep in beach. 'I don't see nothin' but sand?'

Spangles dropped his spade and ran after Freddie, who was sprinting across the beach towards the sea. He waved the hat frantically at the fast-approaching Coast Guard boat before turning sharply and heading along the shoreline.

'Professor! A little help maybeeee,' he shouted over his shoulder at the cave.

'Sausage! Get him!' Spangles yelled for his own fishy reinforcement. But Sausage was still digging and had accidentally buried himself almost up to his middle. **'What's that, me old swear box?'** Sausage replied, looking up and suddenly realising he was stuck.

'ARGHHHHH! HELP! I'M SINKING!' he shrieked.

'I'M SINKING! I'M SINKING!' Jeff repeated, knowing perfectly well he could flap away any time he liked, but he was enjoying himself too much to leave just yet.

Freddie circled the beach and was heading back towards the sea as Splasher Harris landed by Turtle Rock next to the **Jolly Naughty**. 'All aboard!' Mayor Jackson shouted, seeing Freddie waving the precious hat as he ran.

Sausage wriggled like a potato in a hula hoop until he was free of his sandy prison. He ran after Spangles running after Freddie, his sand-filled wellies slowing him down like in one of those running-in-treacle dreams. 'Flippin' treacly dreams,' he complained as he huffed towards his boat.

'**Treacly dreams, treacly dreams,**' Jeff squawked happily, gripping Sausage's mac firmly in his claws.

Freddie leaped aboard the Coast Guard boat and was greeted with a loud cheer from Mayor Jackson. The powerful engine was still running, purring like a kitten. Splasher threw the throttle forward to Topper-most Escape Speed, swapping the purr for a pridely lion roar as they shot out to sea.

Spangles jumped aboard the **Jolly Naughty** and waited for Sausage to catch up. He was so angry, he would have quite happily had a punch-up with a whole pride of lions AND a kitten AND he would have probably won. **'After them, Sausage! After them!'** Spangles screamed as Sausage finally arrived and started the engine. The **Jolly Naughty** chugged away from Smugglers' Cove, slower than trees grow.

Cannon Ball

'**AHARRR!** Freddie, come join your captain in the crow's-nest. **Freddie? . . . Hey!** Where is everyone?' **Professor Bonehead** dropped from the tunnel wall. He marched out of the cave onto the deserted beach in time to see the two boats leaving.

'**SWASHBUCKLING TRAITOR RAT DOGS!**' he yelled, with as much piracy as his brain could download from his ancestry. He waved a furious fist. **'Leave me marooned on this desert island, would you?! We'll see about that!'** He ran back into the cave and emerged seconds later carrying a bag of gunpowder, a ramrod and a very heavy cannonball.

He quickly loaded the cannon and adjusted its position in the sand to point at the escaping boats. Looking along the barrel, he squinted one-eyed at the **Jolly Naughty** chugging away in the cannon's firing line. With one final, **'AHARRR!'** he lit the short fuse.

Professor Bonehead stood back as it fizzed to life briefly before exploding with a powerful bang, hurling its cannonball cargo out to sea.

Spangles and Sausage heard the bang. They spun round and stared in horror at the cannonball whizzing towards them.

They looked up **speechlessly** as it shot by, barely three feet over their heads.

And they watched in happy hysterics as it **crashed** down onto the Coast Guard boat ahead of them.

Splasher Harris, being a hopeless swimmer but a sensible sailor, had taken the precaution of inviting his inflatable friends to the chase. These consisted of a large inflatable jacket, an inflatable ring the size of a tractor tyre, armbands, and legbands.

When the cannonball struck it crashed right through his boat from deck to hull in seconds, causing it to lurch sideways and **flipping** Mayor Jackson, Freddie, Splasher and his inflatable friends high into the air and overboard.

'Oh flip!' Splasher said, rather accurately, as he sailed skywards and flipped over, splashing down feet-first nearby, closely followed by a splosh from Mayor Jackson and a sploosh from Freddie.

SPLOSH!

SPLOOSH!

SPLASH!

As Freddie surfaced, he realised his T-shirt was flapping about freely in the water with nothing at all stuffed beneath it.

Sausage and Spangles cheered as they chugged closer to the wreckage. Jeff said nothing. He had enjoyed the sweary singing and the digging and running, but didn't think there was anything at all funny about boats being sunk by cannonballs.

When Spangles spotted something spangly floating amongst the debris of the sinking boat, his eyebrows did a handstand. He grabbed Sausage by the collar of his once-yellow-now-black fisherman's mac and screamed, 'HAT! HAT! HAT!' It sounded like the weirdest laugh ever.

'Fishing net!' Sausage shouted back, steering towards the **Diamond Skull** as it began slipping beneath the waves. Spangles released his grip of Sausage and instead got a grip of the net Sausage was pointing at.

All the shouting was beginning to annoy Jeff. **'For goodness sake, people!'** he squawked, flapping up from Sausage's shoulder. **'Can't a parrot perch in peace!'**

He circled the **Jolly Naughty**, his hopes for freedom rising with each feathery flippity flap until he saw, glinting in the sunlight, the hat that seemed to be causing all the fuss. He swooped down, grabbed it in his beak and flapped back towards the **piratey boat** and the two strange weirdos he'd come to know as . . . two strange weirdos.

Jeff had every intention of returning the hat to them before he left and was right above the boat when the taller one started shouting, **'Why did you keep that stupidy, stupidy, idiot parrot?!'**

Sausage laddered quickly up to the **Jolly Naughty's** recently added crow's-nest, stood on his tippiest toes and stretched his longest to reach Jeff and the **Diamond Skull**.

But he was too late. Jeff had a change of heart and a change of direction, and **flapped** away.

He would have said goodbye, but that would have meant dropping the hat and he quite fancied keeping hold of it for a bit. He headed for the

169

sun-filled horizon, like in all the best happy endings, in search of new hatty adventures.

Professor Bonehead shuffled slowly back to his cannon, carrying a second cannonball from the cave. **'You won't escape Captain Bonehead that easily!'** he shouted. He re-loaded the cannon and lit the fuse.

A second bang echoed around the cove as another badly aimed cannonball whooshed seawards and flew over the **Jolly Naughty** without even bothering to slow down to wave at the waves.

Unaware of the incoming cannonball, Jeff got quite a shock when it shot past, clipping his flapping wings, causing him to lose a few of his favourite feathers. He squawked,

170

'Why don't you watch where you're going?'

This in turn caused him to drop the hat. He watched his new spangly hat fall down towards the sea.

Then he flapped onwards happily. 'Oh well, hats they come and hats they go,' he said, all philosophy and dreams.

Gravity is super strong and invisible, like two superheroes in one. It has been around for a long time, even longer than diamonds, and some of *them* have been hanging around sparkling for three billion years.

Gravity was thinking about this as it grabbed the famous hat and pulled it down with its own very particular force. Its attention was suddenly taken by a speeding cannonball which was quickly running out of physics and also in need of gravity's assistance, so it stopped thinking about diamonds and got to grips with plunging cannonballs into the sea instead.

Spangles didn't take his eyes off the falling hat. **'Sausage! That way!'** he pointed towards the horizon, not especially helpfully. Sausage was already sliding back down the mast to the poop deck where he thrust the throttle to Top Chugging Speed and shouted over his shoulder to Freddie, Mayor Jackson and Splasher Harris, **'So long, losers!'** as the **Jolly Naughty** sailed away into a treasure-seeking future.

Freddie had watched the **plucky parrot** peck the hat from the sea and saw the second cannonball knock it from its cheeky beak moments later. As Spangles and Sausage chugged away, he started laughing and almost swallowed a lungful of sea water as he shouted after them, 'Please don't leave us!'

'I really don't see what's so funny, Freddie,' Mayor Jackson snapped.

'Me neither!' added Splasher Harris. He was almost in tears as bits of his **beloved** boat sank around him.

Freddie waited until the **Jolly Naughty** was far away enough before raising his left hand triumphantly above the waves. In his hand was the real **Diamond Skull pirate hat**, which he'd been holding onto very tightly since **snatching** it off Spangles' naughty head.

Splasher Harris lent Freddie and the Mayor Jackson his inflatable rubber ring, and they all swam slowly back to the beach.

When they had retold the whole story to **Professor Bonehead**, and **Professor Bonehead** had apologised repeatedly to Splasher Harris for accidentally sinking his boat, a moment of calm descended over the cove.

'We should probably get this hat back to the museum and re-open your exhibition, Mayor,' **Professor Bonehead Junior Junior** suggested.

Mayor Jackson didn't answer for a moment. His gaze was fixed on the tiny silhouette of the **Jolly Naughty** in the distance. He was considering calling Chief Nutter again and reporting the theft and the thieves, but that would involve explaining exactly what had happened to the real **Diamond Skull** and he was having a far better, tourism-raising idea about that.

'So out there in the bay somewhere, is definitely one hat . . . Correct?' he asked.

'Definitely,' Freddie replied.

'But it's a fake. And the real one . . . **the real Diamond Skull** . . . well, sadly it was lost at sea in a heroic struggle between Mayor Jackson, Coast Guard Splasher Harris, local hero Freddie Taylor and the rather nasty Spangles McNasty and his ridiculous sausage-faced friend.'

'**Well . . . no, it's here . . .**' the Professor replied,

pointing to the hat the Mayor himself was now holding.

'It is believed a fake hat may also be lost at sea in Bitterly Bay, but no reward will be offered for that. Only the return of the genuine **Diamond Skull** will be met with a handsome reward,' the Mayor continued, without taking his eyes off the distant fishing boat.

'Oh, I see,' Freddie said. 'An enormous reward might sound better, though?'

'Hmm? Yes, yes, of course. An enormously, massive, huge reward! Right as always, Freddie.' The Mayor laughed and threw his arms around Freddie and the Professor. Unfortunately for Splasher Harris, Mayor Jackson only had two arms so Splasher didn't get a hug, which he thought was a little unfair as no one else's boat had been sunk from under them.

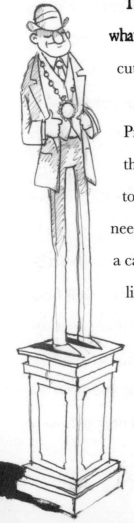

'I'm sorry, Mayor, I really don't know what . . .' the Professor began but was cut short by Mayor Jackson.

'Aha! And that, my dear Professor, is because you are all about the past, where as *I* am all about tomorrow! And tomorrow, we'll be needing more tourists, won't we? With a carefully worded press release and a little fibbing, we'll have treasure lost at sea in Bitterly Bay and a huge reward! Oh my, oh my, they really will have to put a statue of me on the promenade for this one!'

If the sun could have smiled it would have done so as it **beamed** down on Smugglers' Cove, it did like a happy ending.

It turned its gaze a little further out to sea, to see two of the most unusual deep-sea divers it had ever encountered.

Onboard the **Jolly Naughty**, Spangles McNasty and Sausage-face Pete had made themselves swimming shorts from the **Jolly Naughty**'s flag and ten-foot-long snorkels from drinking straws. They were poised ready to jump. **'You sure this'll work, Sausage?'** Spangles asked.

'You know what they say, me old treasure hunt,' Sausage scratched his **fake** whiskers thoughtfully. 'So much is there to see, a drop in the ocean is blue, like the sea.' Feeling this was a fitting sentence to end the day's shenanigans and also that it was wise and wonderful, honest and true, he jumped overboard.

The sun watched another splash as Spangles joined him.

It had been a *tiring* day. But what a day! One to tell the grandchildren about, the sun thought and then remembered it was the sun and couldn't tell stories, or have grandchildren.

When it woke the following morning, it decided to have a lie-in and let old windy gusts have a go at being the weather for a bit. Windy gusts loved *blowing* all the fluffy clouds about so much, the sun asked it to stay all week.

A week in which Freddie *scrapped* his **pirate** project homework and wrote something far better about tourism in seaside towns and how it could be surprisingly *exciting*.

Captain Crumples started a twelve-year course in Advanced Mathematics and Accounting.

Sergeant Pickles had an overwhelming

response to her advert in the **Bitterly Daily Blah Blah** for her new night class in Mixed Martial Ceramic Arts: *Kara-potty – A smashing combination of karate and pottery.*

Marjory decided enough was enough and made an appointment with a therapist called Doctor Von-Key Bonks about her addiction to **SPOOKY COOKY**.

The Best Beach Award judges had a right laugh at Bitterly Beach which was still being dug up by two hundred treasure-seekers when they arrived on Sunday.

Professor Bonehead Junior Junior went home and hid his priceless **pirate hat** safely in his safe. As promised, he told no one about this and even did a little fib to the press which backed up Mayor Jackson's own report about the hat being lost at sea.

Mayor Jackson gave a passionate speech from the museum steps about the disappearance of the **Diamond Skull** and detailed the huge, enormous and massive reward he would give for its return.

It was also a week in which Spangles McNasty found the fake **Diamond Skull**, washed up on the little beach by the lighthouse at Rock Bank. He recognised his own handiwork at once and after a shouting match with Philip Go-Lightly, the very vocal lighthouse keeper, he decided to let Philip keep it.

It was at this precise, fed-uply moment that Spangles McNasty realised they were going to need something a little better than ten-foot-long straws to help them search the entire underwater area of Bitterly Bay and find the real **Diamond Skull** before anyone else did.

'**Something a bit more . . . you know . . . nautical,**' he said to Sausage as they sailed away from Rock Bank.

'**Naughty?**' Sausage replied.

'**No, no, like science, you know.** Underwater science. **Like electric sharks,**' Spangles said, trying to explain his peculiar thinking.

'**Oh, like a shark-shaped submarine!**' Sausage

said. 'My grandfather built one once, a **Great White one it was**. In the past. **When he was alive.** And also when he was a marine biologist or something.'

'Yes, Sausage!' Spangles shouted louder than even he had expected, such was his surprise at his friend's hidden depths.

'Still got it. In me shed.' Sausage explained.

'You've got a shed?'

'Doesn't everyone?' Sausage replied.

'With a **great white shark-shaped submarine** in it?'

'Doesn't everyone? Ha! Only kidding. But, yeah, I have, as it happens. **Think it'll be useful?'**

Spangles looked around at the bright, **shimmering** sea, **squinted** up at the sun and smiled. Spangles liked the sun. He liked the way it made all of his favourite shiners sparkle when it shone its happy heat on them. He sometimes wondered if it was watching him, and what it thought about all day.

'Well, me old sunshine, you know what I think?' he waited a polite second or two for the sun to reply, but the sun wasn't listening, it was busy playing in the shadows. **'This is going to be a right super SPANGLER of a day,'** Spangles grinned. **'I can just feel it.'**

THE END

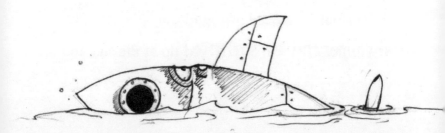

Spangles McNasty and the Fish of Gold

Steve Webb

Illustrated by Chris Mould

Spangles McNasty is convinced that he can get rich quick by stealing goldfish – after all, aren't they made of solid gold? Together with his friend Sausage-face Pete, he decides to find the great Fish of Gold. Only young Freddie Taylor can stop Spangles' dastardly plan, in a tale full of time-travelling jet skis, madcap chases and haunted custard.

'Unadulterated fun!'
Lovereading

'Ludicrous and funny'
BookTrust

9781783444007   £6.99

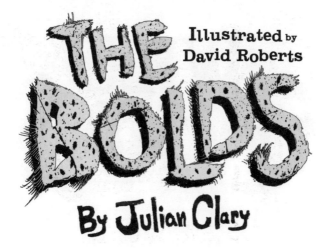

THE BOLDS

Illustrated by David Roberts

By Julian Clary

The Bolds are just like you and me: they live in a house, they have jobs and they love to have a bit of a giggle. But this family has one great big hairy secret – they're hyenas.

So far, the Bolds have managed to keep things under wraps. But the nosy man next door smells a rat. Will the Bolds be able to keep their secret safe?

'Joyful' *Telegraph*
'Glorious' *Daily Mail*
'Heaps of fun' *Heat*

9781783443055   £6.99

DEREK KEILTY

ILLUSTRATED BY JONNY DUDDLE

It's time for revenge!

Will Gallows, a young elfling sky cowboy, is riding out on a dangerous quest. His mission? To bring Noose Wormworx, the evil snake-bellied troll, to justice. Noose is wanted for the murder of Will's pa, and Will won't stop until he's got revenge!

'Wow, what a brilliant read. Fresh and original – and very funny too.'
Joseph Delaney, author of *The Spook's Apprentice*

9781849392365 £6.99

THE DRAGONSITTER DISASTERS

JOSH LACEY

Illustrated by Garry Parsons

Dear Uncle Morton,
You'd better get on a plane right now and come
back here. Your dragon has eaten Jemima.

When Eddie agrees to look after his uncle's
dragon, he soon realises it's not going to be as
easy as he'd thought.

From blazing curtains and missing
pets to a firework catastrophe,
this fabulously funny collection
of three Dragonsitter stories will
have you roaring for more!

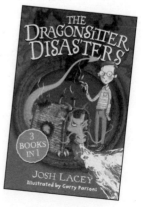

9781783441228 £6.99